Partridge

A Michael Grey short story - 10

Isabella Muir

Happy reading

Isabella

x

OUTSET

OUTSET PUBLISHING LTD

Published in Great Britain

By Outset Publishing Ltd

First edition published December 2023

ISBN: 978-1-872889-67-2

www.isabellamuir.com

Contents

By the same author

GIUSEPPE BIANCHI MYSTERIES

Featuring retired Italian detective - Giuseppe Bianchi
CROSSING THE LINE *
AFTER THE STORM *

JANIE JUKE MYSTERIES

Featuring young librarian and amateur sleuth - Janie Juke
BOOK 1: THE TAPESTRY BAG *
BOOK 2: LOST PROPERTY *
BOOK 3: THE INVISIBLE CASE *
BOOK 4: A NOTABLE OMISSION

THE SUSSEX CRIME MYSTERIES

A Janie Juke trilogy - box set

SUSSEX MYSTERY NOVELLAS
Featuring characters from the Janie Juke novels
DIVIDED WE FALL
MORE THAN ASHES
WAITING FOR SUNSHINE
THE HARVEST
CHOICES
NEVER ENOUGH

THE FORGOTTEN CHILDREN *
A story about a mother's search for her child

TWELVE AT CHRISTMAS
An anthology of twelve Christmas-themed short stories

IVORY VELLUM
An anthology of short stories

*Also available as an audiobook.
www.isabellamuir.com

1960

Christmas Eve...

...and a partridge in a pear tree...

Introducing...

I've been on a wonderful imaginary journey while writing this series of short stories, mapping the life of Michael Grey and meeting his family and friends.

This has been a fascinating series to write. With each story new characters seem to present themselves, as if they have knocked on my front door to say hello. Each person who has cropped up in the series has his or her own back story, leaving plenty for me to explore in the future.

As well as meeting new characters, writing the stories has given me a chance to learn about birds, wildlife and nature. I've discovered more about the history and folklore associated with my birthplace – St Leonards-on-Sea in Sussex, and its surroundings. Nearby Hastings will be familiar to many from school history lessons, with 1066 – the date of the Battle of Hastings - etched into our memories. Over the centuries

Hastings has been associated with a whole host of famous people, too many to list here. It was the place John Logie Baird (said to be the inventor of television) carried out many of his initial experiments; where novelist Catherine Cookson lived and wrote many of her stories; and where poet and illustrator, Daniel Gabriel Rossetti lived, worked and married.

Characters and setting merge with nature in this series, and, of course, my passion for all aspects of the iconic era of the 1960s.

Michael Grey has been the ideal character to lead these stories. He is a young man who discovers that so many of the characteristics and habits of the birds he loves to watch are reflected in the people closest to him, his family and friends.

We've followed Michael Grey through December 1960, at the beginning of a decade that saw a host of significant changes, many that still resonate today. It was a decade when young people were finding their voice and older people were struggling to come to terms with the newly defined 'generation gap'.

Some say the 'swinging sixties' really took off in 1964, the year that saw the Beatles rise to international fame, but it was 1960 when the group first got together, playing sessions in the now world-famous Cavern Club in Liverpool by 1961. An explosion of talent emerged during the next few years, with a whole host of pop and rock artists, many whose music is just as popular today.

Mary Quant, among others, transformed the way that young people dressed, as interior designers, such as Terence Conran, transformed how many people furnished their homes, making contemporary furniture available at affordable prices.

As well as music and fashion, the growth of consumerism

and the widespread availability of labour-saving devices meant people had more leisure time to enjoy.

Aside from the changes that a strengthening youth culture brought about, Britain began to see the problems brought about by intensive farming, with nature beginning to suffer. We see the longer term effects now, with our loss of wildlife habitats and the very real fears about climate change.

It was also the decade when car ownership took off, with estimates suggesting the numbers of people owning cars rose during the decade from around nine million to fifteen million. Thinking back to my childhood, I recall so few cars passed by our house there was no danger for me to cross the road on my own at the tender age of eight. And yet, that same road now sees tens of thousands of vehicles pass along it every day, with young and old taking their life in their hands should they decide to venture from one side to the other.

It's interesting to see how events during that decade, as well as the social and political changes that occurred, formed a springboard to launch much that has happened subsequently.

Researching for historical fiction has taken me on a fascinating journey. I hope, in turn, the results of that research, as played out in this series of stories, will take you on a journey that is just as magical.

Happy reading!

Partridge

The rain over the last few days had been relentless. Parts of Ecclesbourne Glen, the huge gash cut into the cliff-line towering over Hastings Old Town, had been threatened by multiple cliff falls. Torrential rain was causing crumbling sandstone to land on the shingle beach below.

On crisp winter days the Glen offered a haven for ramblers who could enjoy walking the paths, following the trickling streams, pausing beside the gentle waterfalls. Locals likened the wooded areas, abundant with ferns and fungi of every kind, to a cold rainforest. But during the worst downpours the streams became rivers, overspilling their banks, soaking the ground around them, making it unpleasant for anyone brave enough to venture out.

Michael Grey had walked the Glen on many occasions, fascinated to see the way wild flowers clung to the cliff face, so delicate and yet so strong. In autumn if he was lucky enough to catch it just right, he'd see the spectacular migrations of swallows and house martins. He'd watched falcons hovering over the tree tops, sweeping down to snatch their prey. It was a dramatic sight but one that left him feeling a little unsettled. One creature capturing another.

This Christmas Eve morning, as he walked to work at Warrior Square station, Ecclesbourne Glen was on his mind. Penelope's return from London had sparked a whole host of memories. Five years had passed since he'd last seen her and so much had changed. The vibrant, pretty girl with the long, blonde hair he'd dated before he headed off to his stint of National Service, had returned from London with even more confidence. It wasn't just the change to her hairstyle, now cropped tight to frame her face. It was the way she carried herself with such poise; she was still effervescent like the best champagne, but somehow she had grown into herself.

He'd changed too, of course. Perhaps even more so during these last few weeks as he discovered truths about the people around him he'd seemingly been blind to.

But for today his thoughts were on Penelope. Or Penny as she now liked to be called. When they'd dated back in their teenage years, they'd often catch the bus into Hastings Old Town on Sunday afternoon, enjoy a ride on the funicular railway up to the West Hill cliffs and from there take a walk over Ecclesbourne Glen. He'd point out the birds and other wildlife they spotted along the way, hoping to impress her with his knowledge about their individual characteristics, listening out for their birdsong.

His job back then, at Kirby's Furniture Emporium, was the best kind of work. All the time he was earning money he was learning. There wasn't much that Mr Kirby didn't know about birds and Penny was a good listener.

In turn, Penny recounted stories about a hermit who was reported to have lived in a cave, tucked away in the upper end of the glen.

'His name was John,' she told Michael. 'He wasn't harming anyone, it's just that he wanted to live a different life. Nothing wrong with that, is there?'

Michael had heard the story before, but he liked to listen to her recounting it as each time she would add something new.

'It was at the turn of the century when he made a home for himself in the cave, feeding himself from an allotment he'd developed over the years he was there. Apparently he'd been in the drapery trade in London, curtains and such like, but he lost everything, ended up bankrupt and that's when he came to Hastings. Locals called him the East Hill hermit. Some say he had quite a refined look about him, not dirty, and always wearing a cloth cap. But this is the bit you'll like, Mickey. He rarely spoke to anyone, but he could often be heard singing to himself, echoing the birdsong that kept him company maybe?'

'Do you think he was happy?' Michael tried to imagine how it would be, with just nature for company.

'Well, we won't ever know for sure, will we? But I like to think he was. He lived a simple life and died a simple death there in the cave, like he'd just gone to sleep. And beside him were piles of books. Stories that had taken him off to places he would never visit, that he didn't need to visit because he'd travelled there through the pages of a book.'

Michael had been so engrossed in the memories of Penny's stories that he'd reached Warrior Square without barely a thought for anything he'd passed along the way. Usually he kept an eye out for a robin nestled in a holly bush, or a row of blue tits perched on a fence, but today they had all gone unnoticed.

The heavy rain that had caused such damage along the Hastings cliffs had moved east a day ago. Now only puddles remained to remind Michael that all week he'd trudged through the rainstorms, hoping his railway boots would last another winter and not let him down. No rain today, but hardly Christmas weather, the frosty scenes that appeared on greetings cards, snow-laden branches, red-nosed reindeers, and the ubiquitous robin picking at a berry, or perching on a letterbox, were nowhere to be seen. Instead the day had started with a grey, leaden sky and a damp chill that threatened to seep through his overcoat. No matter, as soon as he arrived at work he'd share an early brew with Bert in the ticket office.

'Morning,' Bert said, not looking up from his copy of the *Daily Mail.* 'Not so wet today, eh?'

Bert lived just a short walk from the station and although he was nearing retirement, Michael wouldn't have been surprised to see him still turn up for work, such was the routine that had seen Bert through forty years or more.

'Thought I'd grab an early brew with you,' Michael said, spooning sugar into his mug. 'You working tomorrow, Bert?'

Christmas Day saw a reduced service, nevertheless, people still had to get about, with most relying on buses and trains to reach their loved ones. Of course, for staff choosing to work overtime it meant a handsome bonus, especially this year, with Christmas Day falling on a Sunday.

'I'll do a half day. It's a chance to get away from my Sylvie with all her fussing and new-fangled recipes. You can't beat tradition, young Michael, you mark my words.'

'Your daughter likes to experiment?'

'Short cuts is what she likes. The other Saturday evening, do you know what she served up for pudding? Instant Whip, she called it, something and nothing in a glass dish. I ask you, what's wrong with a nice homemade apple pie, eh?'

Instant Whip was a recent favourite for Michael. He loved the idea of just having to empty the packet of powder into a bowl, add some milk, mix it with a fork and a minute later he had a satisfying pudding. But he sensed that sharing his opinion on the popular convenience food with Bert, whose likes and dislikes centred wholly on tradition, would not end well.

'Here, this is for you,' Bert said, handing over an envelope.

'Ah, Bert, thanks. I didn't think we did Christmas cards. I haven't got one for you.'

'It's not from me, lad. A pretty little thing came in first thing, I'd not even sold a ticket it was so early. She comes up to the window and I'm ready to ask her where she's travelling to so early on Christmas Eve, when she gives me a great big smile and hands me this envelope. "Would you mind giving this to Mickey Grey for me," she says, polite as anything. "You mean young Michael," I said. She nods and then she says, bold as you like, "And I wish you a very happy Christmas, Mr Ticket Clerk," and with that she was gone, leaving behind her a wonderful scent of carnations and lilies. Took me right back it did, reminded me of the perfume my Rose wore.

'Your wife?'

'They knew what they were doing when they named her, that's for sure. Just like a rose she was, so delicate, with skin so smooth and fine, she didn't need any of that muck the young girls put on their faces nowadays.'

Michael was still holding the envelope, desperate to open it to discover its contents, but not wanting to deter Bert from his reminiscing.

'Was she blonde?" Michael asked.

'No, not at all. Her hair was as black as can be, raven black you'd call it. And not a strand of grey right up until the day she died.'

It was going to be awkward to retrace the steps that had led to a confusion in their conversation, with Bert thinking about his wife and Michael thinking only about Penny.

'Well, I'd better get on. The Hastings train is due any minute. But thanks for this, Bert,' Michael said, waving the envelope at his colleague before stepping out onto the platform.

There wasn't time to look at the card, at least if he opened it now he would be rushed and he wanted to savour the moment. *Ridiculous. It's hardly a momentous occasion, receiving a Christmas card from an old friend.* Nevertheless, he would choose his moment.

Quite a number of passengers alighted from the Hastings train, some laden with parcels, others with shopping bags overloaded with food. He helped a few of them negotiate the opening and closing of the heavy train carriage doors as they shifted their parcels and bags from one hand to another. Plenty thanked him with a Christmas greeting, others with a nod of the head. One family of four was the last to make their way along the platform towards the exit. The man and woman each carried a heavy suitcase, the two young boys held hands.

'Could you help us to a taxi, Porter?' the man called out.

Michael gestured to the family to follow him out through the ticket office to the taxi rank where two taxis were waiting. He took the suitcase from the woman, lifting it into the boot of the taxi, before turning to help the man with his case.

'*Grazie*,' the woman said, quickly turning away and sliding into the taxi, gathering her children onto the seat beside her.

'You're from Italy?' Michael said.

'We have just arrived on the boat train from France. My wife is Italian,' the man said, as if that was explanation enough.

Michael had read about the night train that ran between London Victoria and Paris, he'd even seen pictures of it, but had never seen it up close. The distinctive blue and gold coaches provided sleeping accommodation for passengers, as well as a buffet car, restaurant, and kitchen. He'd always imagined how luxurious it would be to travel through the night, to go to sleep in England and wake up in France.

'Well, a very happy Christmas to you,' Michael said, closing the taxi door, wondering briefly where the family would spend their Christmas. With family perhaps, or friends? Would Hastings be their new home, or were they here for a short visit? Time and again the people he encountered so briefly during his working day left him wondering, but the chances were he would never see them again.

It was mid morning before he had a quiet moment to look at the envelope, which he had slipped into his railway bag to keep it safe and dry. It was addressed simply to, *Mickey,* and below his name a drawing in red crayon of a bird in flight. The picture on the front of the card was of two robins sitting on top of a snow-covered lamp-post. He'd last seen Penny ten days ago. They'd sat in one of the seafront shelters and a robin had settled on a nearby lamp-post, singing its heart out. He could almost hear the robins on the front of the card doing the self-same thing.

As he opened the card to read the message, a postcard fell out. The Christmas card carried a simple greeting: *Happy Christmas, Mickey.* She'd signed it *Penny,* with one kiss. The image on the front of the postcard was a sepia photograph of Lover's Seat, the date beneath it 1910. On the seat sat a lady in all her Edwardian finery, a ruffled blouse atop a long skirt, a wide-brimmed hat, holding a walking stick in her right hand. On the reverse of the postcard Penny had written: *Meet me at here at six.*

He slid the cards back in the envelope, slipping it into his overcoat pocket. Around now he would usually take a tea break, a chance to chat with Bert, but he wasn't in the mood for Bert's chatter. He wanted to reflect on the card and its message and for that he needed to be on his own. There were no trains due in from either direction for another ten minutes, giving him a chance to enjoy the relative warmth of the waiting room. The two-bar electric fire was turned on for an hour early mornings on bitterly cold days, but it did little to raise the temperature. Staff weren't really supposed to use the room, but Michael would only be in trouble if the Station Master turned up. An unlikely occurrence on Christmas Eve. Station Master Reynolds was based at Hastings Station, making the occasional trip to the smaller nearby stations like Warrior Square, West St Leonards, and Ore. In his absence Bert filled the role of Assistant Station Master, although it was a post in name only as Bert rarely left the comfort of his ticket office.

Taking the cards from his pocket, Michael read the message again to see if the picture or the few words on the reverse of the postcard would give him a clue as to Penny's thoughts when she wrote it. It was strange that she should have chosen Lover's Seat for their meeting, when just that morning he'd been thinking about the same place. It had been a regular stop off for them during their walks over Ecclesbourne Glen. Another place where Penelope regaled him with tales from the past. The simple wooden bench stood on a precarious cliff ledge high above the beach below. In years past it provided the perfect look-out spot for smugglers bringing in tea, tobacco and spirits from France, traded for Sussex wool and even live sheep. Smuggling was rife all along the Sussex coast, with the glen providing plenty of hideaways for the guilty to escape capture.

There were all sorts of stories about the seat itself. According to Penny, some said the seat gained its name from a lovers' tryst in the seventeen hundreds, the place where a couple met in secret, defying the wishes of their families.

'It's so romantic, don't you think?' Penelope had said. 'Just imagine. He would arrive on the beach below, scramble up the cliffs and there she would be, just waiting for him.'

'Not so easy to scramble up or down those cliffs now,' Michael said, looking down over the gorse and bracken cliff face below them.

'You know it's in a famous painting by Holman Hunt, don't you? When I'm in London I'll visit the Tate Gallery and stand in front of that painting and think about this moment, of you and I sitting on this very seat.'

Now, as he sat in the station waiting room, looking at Penny's note, he wondered if she'd visited the gallery, if she'd stood in front of the painting and if she'd given a moment's thought to their time together.

Of course, the bench they sat on when they were dating wasn't the same piece of timber that was there when the ill-fated lovers met, or the one that Holman Hunt had depicted. Over the centuries it had been destroyed and replaced many times. Where Penelope had gathered her stories from about this little piece of Hastings history Michael could only guess. Perhaps delving into the archives at the public library, or maybe she'd conjured up the tales from her imagination. Whether it was fact or fiction, Michael loved to listen to her excited chatter.

'Then in the twenties a group of thugs lifted the bench

up and just threw it off the cliff,' she told him. 'Only these three little stumps were left.' She bent down to examine them. 'They fitted a new seat, but in the war it was destroyed again and a lovely local person donated the trunk of an oak tree for someone to fashion a new seat. And they put it in place on Valentine's Day, so you see it's always been connected with love and romance.'

At the time, when Michael listened to Penny's stories, he thought little about them. But now he wondered what it was she was really saying.

The rest of the day dragged, he looked at his watch endlessly, with every ten minutes feeling like an hour had passed. His shift ended at four. He'd get home as fast as possible, change out of his uniform, then catch the bus into Hastings. A hastily made sandwich would keep him going, that and a glass of milk.

By the time he was sitting on the top deck of the No 465 bus, he was wishing he'd made time to buy Penny a Christmas present. A week ago he'd spent an hour or so searching the shop windows for inspiration as to what to buy his parents. In the end he chose a pair of leather gloves for his dad and a silk scarf for his mum. Both gifts likely to be tucked into a drawer and kept 'for best'.

And Penny? He'd written her a card, which was in his duffel coat pocket, next to the card she'd left for him that morning. But a Christmas present? Perhaps he'd get something from one of the Old Town shops if they were still open.

The bus seemed to be taking forever. By the time they reached the halfway mark on the journey, the top deck was already full. The conductor stopped calling out, *Plenty of room up top,* instead telling the passengers down below to *Move along there, please.* As the bus passed the bottom of

London Road, Michael glanced out of the window and was sure he saw Penny's cherry red Mini pass by. He almost went to wave, before realising he was being ridiculous. In fact, he was being more than ridiculous, reading too much into the simple invitation from one old friend to another.

Just before his stop, he rang the bell, queuing behind several other passengers who were all alighting at the foot of the East Hill lift. Grateful the lift was still running, Michael sat alone in the little railway car as it journeyed up the cliff face. Taking the ride on a bright summer's day up the steepest funicular railway in the country, meant the chance to enjoy spectacular views over the Old Town, the tall black wooden fishing huts and the beach beyond. But now, late on Christmas Eve, it was just the sparkle from the few strings of Christmas lights, strung from lamppost to lamppost that broke up the darkness.

Once up on the hill it was a twenty-minute walk to the cliff top, a little over a mile of muddy footpaths. Meeting in such a precarious place was crazy enough in the daytime, but on a winter's evening, after days of heavy rainfall, it was surely madness. One slip for either would see them tumbling down the cliff face to spend Christmas Day in hospital, or worse. But that had always been Penny's way, forever challenging the possible.

No surprise that he didn't pass another soul on his walk across the glen. In the gloom, with just his torchlight for company, he thought of the old hermit who'd lived in the nearby cave. How must it have been for him, living such a solitary life? Would he have enjoyed the birdsong that Michael was enjoying now, a soundtrack for his walk. A robin, a song thrush, a blackbird, and an owl. He could pick out each of their voices, individual parts of an orchestra, who seemed to be taking it in turn to sing.

He kept the beam from the torch pointed down at the ground just ahead of him, occasionally shining it forward to make sure he didn't lose sight of the path, or stumble into a gorse bush. It was just as he neared Lover's Seat that he saw her. She'd arrived before him. Beside her on the bench was an oil-filled lantern sending shadows in all directions, lighting her face and picking out the red of her corduroy hat, its peak pulled forward over her forehead.

'Mickey, you came,' she called out, not waiting for him to reach her before standing and stepping towards him. 'Look, isn't it pretty?' She pointed at the lantern, then patted the bench beside her. 'Do you remember when we used to come here? All the stories I told you about this place?'

He wanted to take a breath, to slow her down, to enjoy each moment and not let it pass unnoticed.

'I remember all of it. But tonight, here, it's a mad place to be. Weren't you scared walking up here on your own?'

'Why would I be scared?'

He remembered the Christmas card he'd brought for her. No gift though; none of the shops were open. He handed it to her and she tore it open, grabbing his torch and shining it on the picture on the front of the card.

'A partridge in a pear tree, of course,' she said, laughing. 'Who came up with that idea anyway? Have you ever seen a partridge in a pear tree, Mickey?'

He shook his head, wondering again why he had never questioned the words of the Christmas song. He'd seen plenty of partridges, but they were ground-loving birds, not keen to fly even when they had to. The thought of them venturing up into a tree, and a pear tree at that, was fanciful at best.

'Escaping a fox, maybe?' he said.

'Turtle doves, swans, geese, calling birds, whatever they

are, they're all in that carol, aren't they? I remember reading something about the words. It's said to have come from a children's game. Someone starts it off, then it goes round a group and when it comes to your turn you have to repeat all the verses and add the next one. If you can't remember a verse, you're given a forfeit, like this.' She leaned towards him and kissed him on the cheek. 'There, it's so dark I can't even tell if you're blushing. Are you blushing, Mickey?'

'Tell me what we're doing here, Penelope.'

'Penny. I told you, everyone calls me Penny now. We were good mates, weren't we? Well, I'm back now, so...' She paused and he wondered if it was her turn to blush.

'So we could be good mates again?'

'Something like that. Anyway, here, this is for you.' She reached down and pulled a small parcel out from a canvas bag by her feet. 'Happy Christmas, Mickey.'

With the dim light from the lantern he could see the brown paper wrapped around the parcel was covered with silver stars.

'I haven't got you anything,' he said, sounding as pathetic as he felt.

'You can take me dancing. New Year's Eve, how about it?' And then her voice fell to a whisper, 'Ssh, did you hear that?'

'Thunder?'

'No, listen.'

They each held their breath, listening. Then it came again, at first a slow shuffling sound, steadily increasing in speed and volume. Moments later, to accompany the sound, he felt movement below his feet.

'Oh, God, Penny, we need to move now. It's the cliff, it's going to give way.'

Shining the torch ahead of them he grabbed her hand as she in turn grabbed her lantern and bag. With each step along the path to the grassed area set back from the cliff he squeezed her hand so tightly that had she fallen he would surely have been pulled down the cliff face with her.

They were just yards away from the bench when they heard the crash, feeling the ground shudder. He shone the torchlight back towards where they had been sitting, to see the sandstone crumbling and falling away, taking with it Lover's Seat, which once more was to fall onto the shingle below.

'Oh, Mickey. Our seat, it's gone.'

'We could have been gone too, that was a close call.'

It was too dark to see her expression, but he could hear the sadness in her voice.

'Let's get out of here, before anything else happens,' he said.

They walked in silence back down towards Barley Lane where her Mini was parked.

'It was supposed to be a fun thing, something special for Christmas,' she said. 'Now it's all spoilt.' She got into the driver's seat, leaving Michael to slide into the passenger seat beside her. And then, as if filled with a new resolve, she said, 'The lantern worked well, though, don't you think?'

'You find the good in everything, don't you?'

'Well, there's no point being miserable, that doesn't get anyone anywhere, does it?'

The car was parked close to a lamppost which threw enough of a glow to light up her face. The walk, the scare they had, and the chill of the night air, all bringing a flush to her cheeks.

'Well, aren't you going to open your present?'

With the clifftop drama still at the forefront of his mind, he'd almost forgotten the parcel he'd tucked into the cavernous pocket of his duffel coat.

'Should I? I mean shouldn't I wait until tomorrow?'

'Absolutely not. I want to see your face when you open it.'

He picked at the Sellotape, trying not to tear the star-covered paper.

'I'm a ripper, I can never wait,' she said. 'I guess you've always been the cautious type. But that's okay, that's why we get on, because we're different.'

She said it so simply, as if it was the most natural thing in the world to say. They got on, yes, of course. They always had. And the five-year gap made no difference at all.

'A transistor radio?' he said, having unwrapped the parcel and reached the box inside. 'Crikey, that must have cost you loads of money. It's too much, too big a present.'

'Now you can listen to Radio Luxembourg every night, Mickey. You'll get to hear the newest sounds, you're just going to love it, I know you are.'

'I don't know what to say.'

'Well, don't say anything then. Just kiss me.'

As 1960 drew to a close, it seemed to Michael at that moment that everything was just beginning.

The Birdsong of Michael Grey is a compilation of all ten short stories in the series.

Thanks

Writing is fun, but it can also be a lonely pursuit, which is why having friends to support and encourage is worth everything. Suffice it to say, this series of short stories only exists as a result of the encouragement of my marvellous writing buddy - Arctic crime and thriller writer, Christoffer Petersen.

Alongside Christoffer, I'm lucky to have a wide group of readers who enjoy my stories, who all inspire me to continue writing.

And forever thanks go to my wonderful husband, who leaves me free to fly, just like the birds who feature in these stories.

About the author

Isabella Muir has a fascination for the past – exploring what it was like for families living through the decades from the 1930s through to the 1970s. She is the author of two crime mystery series, both set in Sussex, in the iconic eras of the 1960s and 1970s, as well several novellas set during the Second World War. Researching all aspects of family life in past decades formed the perfect launch pad for her works of fiction. Isabella rediscovered her love of writing fiction during two happy years working on and completing her MA in Professional Writing and since then has gone to publish seven novels, six novellas and two short story collections.

The first series of her ***Sussex Crime Mysteries*** features young librarian and amateur sleuth, Janie Juke. Set in the late 1960s, in the fictional seaside town of Tamarisk Bay, we meet Janie, who looks after the mobile library. She is an avid lover of Agatha Christie stories – in particular Hercule Poirot – using all she has learned from the Queen of Crime to help solve crimes and mysteries. As well as four novels, there are six novellas in the series, which explore some of the back story to the Tamarisk Bay characters.

The setting for the Janie Juke mystery series is based on the area where Isabella was born and lived most of her life. When she thinks of Tamarisk Bay she pictures her birthplace in St Leonards-on-sea, East Sussex and its surroundings.

Her novels, ***Crossing the Line*** and ***After the Storm*** are part of a new series of ***Sussex Crime Mysteries***, introducing retired Italian detective, Giuseppe Bianchi.

Isabella's standalone novel, ***The Forgotten Children***, deals with the emotive subject of the child migrants who were sent to Australia – again focusing on family life in the 1960s, when the child migrant policy was still in force.

Find out more by visiting: **www.isabellamuir.com**

Printed in Great Britain
by Amazon

42390938R00020